D0382239

WE SHALL NOT CEASE FROM
EXPLORATION,
AND THE END OF ALL
OUR EXPLORING WILL BE
TO ARRIVE WHERE WE STARTED
AND KNOW THE PLACE
FOR THE FIRST TIME.

T. S. Eliot

TO MY HAIRY,
UNCIVILIZED FRIEND ERIN,
WITH LOVE.

Copyright © 2016 by Frann Preston-Gannon

Nosy Crow and its logos are trademarks of Nosy Crow Ltd.
Used under license.

Excerpt from "Little Gidding" from *Four Quartets* by T. S. Eliot. Copyright 1936 by Houghton Mifflin Harcourt Publishing Company; copyright © renewed 1964 by T.S. Eliot. Copyright 1940, 1942 by T. S. Eliot; copyright © renewed 1968, 1970 by Esme Valerie Eliot. Reprinted by permission of Houghton Mifflin Harcourt Publishing Company.

All rights reserved. No part of this book may be reproduced, transmitted, or stored in an information retrieval system in any form or by any means, graphic, electronic, or mechanical, including photocopying, taping, and recording, without prior written permission from the publisher.

First U.S. edition 2018

Library of Congress Catalog Card Number pending
ISBN 978-0-7636-9628-3

17 18 19 20 21 22 GBL 10 9 8 7 6 5 4 3 2 1

Printed in Shenzhen, Guangdong, China

This book was typeset in Edbaskerville.
The illustrations were created digitally.

Nosy Crow
an imprint of
Candlewick Press
99 Dover Street
Somerville, Massachusetts 02144

www.nosycrow.com
www.candlewick.com

DAVE'S CAVE

FRANN PRESTON-GANNON

nosy crow™
An imprint of Candlewick Press

WITHDRAWN

This Dave.

This Dave's cave.

Dave **like** cave.
Nice green grass.

Big comfy rocks.
This cave perfect.

Dave's friends
like cave, too.

But Dave **not** happy.
Dave wide awake.

Maybe Dave find **better**
cave with **greener** grass
and **bigger** rocks.

Dave want **new** cave.

Dave put out fire.

Off Dave go.

HOME

But first cave not **quite** right.

Second cave

not cozy like home.

Third cave
too noisy.

Fourth cave nice,
but Dave not like pets.

Fifth cave nice, too . . .
HOME
SWEET
HOME

but Jon **not** like sharing.

Dave sad.

Maybe . . .

no better cave,
with greener grass
and bigger rocks.

But look! This cave nice.

Green grass.

Big rocks.

This
cave
perfect.

This cave . . .

home.

31901061390508